N G   S   T   R   A   I   T

The Diomedes Islands

The Waters of the Change of Days

Yesterday Island

Ignaluk
The Lesser Island

Between the Diomedes Islands lie
the Waters of the Change of Days.
Crossing from one to the other means
a journey to Tomorrow or Yesterday.

Dedication

This book is dedicated to my grandson, Clifford.
He was named after his father's mother's father.

Acknowledgments

Kristin Blackwood

Sage

Vi-yen

Murphy

Mike Blanc

Paul Royer

Kurt Landefeld

Sean Sudduth

Sheila Tarr

FISH-BOY
An Inuit Folk Tale
VanitaBooks, LLC

Illustration and design by Mike Blanc.
Hardcover Edition ISBN 978-1-938164-20-0   Paperback Edition ISBN 978-1-938164-21-7
Printed in China.

VanitaBooks, LLC

www.VanitaBooks.com

Fish-Boy

An Inuit Folk Tale

As told by

Vanita Oelschlager

With art by

Mike Blanc

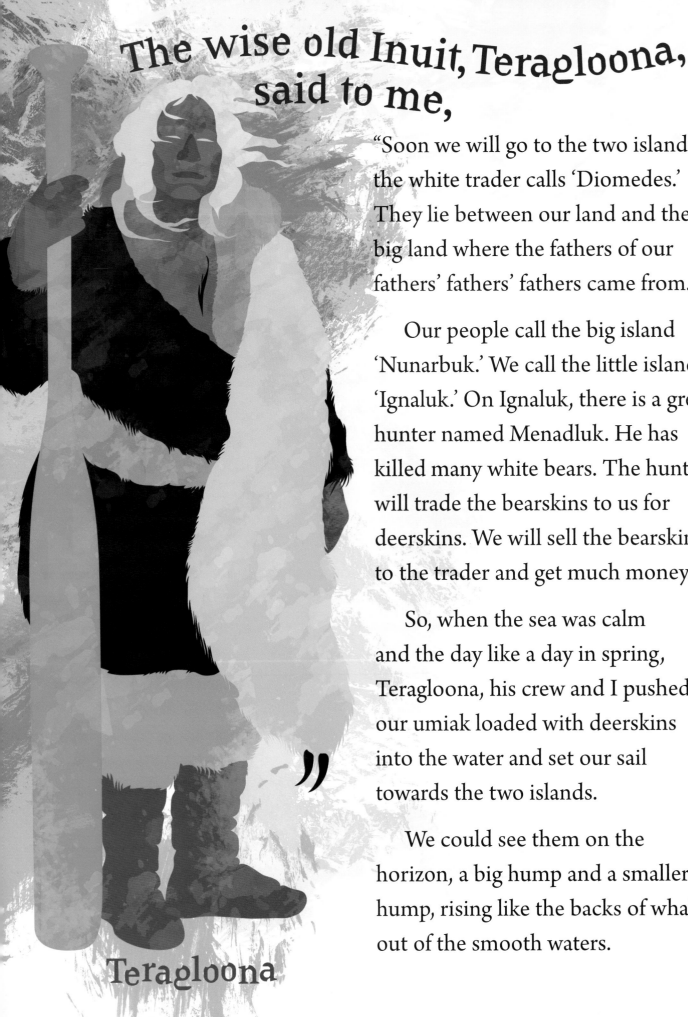

The wise old Inuit, Teragloona, said to me,

"Soon we will go to the two islands the white trader calls 'Diomedes.' They lie between our land and the big land where the fathers of our fathers' fathers' fathers came from.

Our people call the big island 'Nunarbuk.' We call the little island 'Ignaluk.' On Ignaluk, there is a great hunter named Menadluk. He has killed many white bears. The hunter will trade the bearskins to us for deerskins. We will sell the bearskins to the trader and get much money."

So, when the sea was calm and the day like a day in spring, Teragloona, his crew and I pushed our umiak loaded with deerskins into the water and set our sail towards the two islands.

We could see them on the horizon, a big hump and a smaller hump, rising like the backs of whales out of the smooth waters.

Teragloona

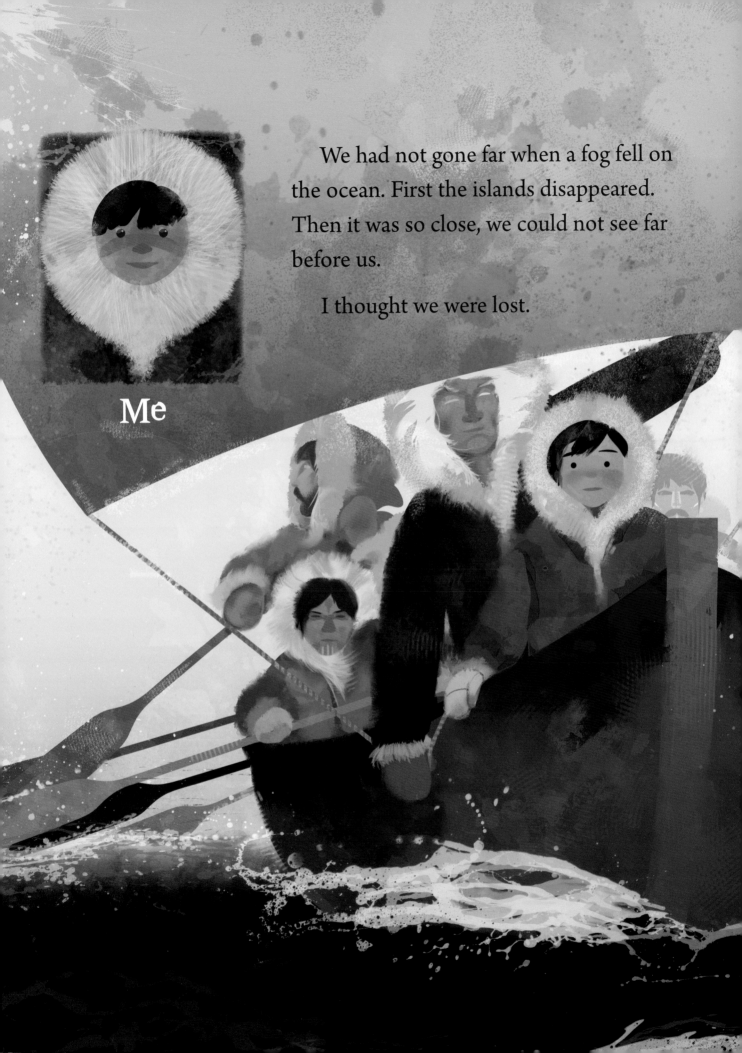

We had not gone far when a fog fell on the ocean. First the islands disappeared. Then it was so close, we could not see far before us.

I thought we were lost.

Me

But wise old Teragloona laughed and shrugged his shoulders. Long years he had lived on the coast of the Arctic. All nature told him things. If the shore would not guide him in his course, the stars beckoned to him or the wind blew him. He told the men to row into the fog as though there was not a cloud in the sky. Because Teragloona knew these waters I lost my fear.

Presently the fog lifted a little and I saw in the distance a shoreline. I thought at first it must be Ignaluk. Lying low against the water, it seemed an endless beach of black sand.

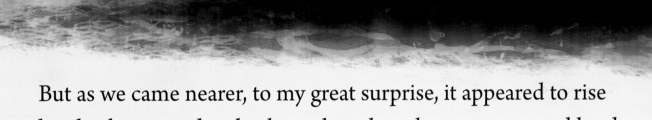

But as we came nearer, to my great surprise, it appeared to rise and go back, rise and go back, so that, though our men rowed hard, we came no closer to it.

"What is that?" I asked, in surprise. "Is this an enchanted isle?"

Teragloona shrugged again and said, "Listen."

I listened, and there came to me a sound as of far distant waterfalls.

"What is it?" I asked.

"Wait." Teragloona bent his shoulders to the paddle. We moved forward in silence.

Finally the fog lifted and I saw it all as one sees after waking from a dream. That which I had thought of as a shoreline was not shoreline, but a million little birds resting on the water. As we came nearer they rose and flew back. Singing as they flew, they made a sound like a waterfall.

"What are they?" I asked.

"Sea-parrots," said Teragloona. "They have nests on Ignaluk, which is a great rock."

"There are so many!" I exclaimed in surprise.

"Like snowflakes in winter. Like stars in the night," said Teragloona.

"Were there always this many?" I asked.

"No, not always. Once there were very few. That, too, is a story. When we get to the island and sit on the bed-shelf in the stone house of the great hunter Menadluk, I will tell you the story."

On Ignaluk all men build their houses of stone, for there are no trees or even driftwood for homes and there are no long poles for houses made of skins.

The Great Hunter

Menadluk

So, before the seal-oil lamp of Menadluk, while I lay stretched out upon a bed of white bearskins, Teragloona told me the story of Fish-Boy and why there are so many sea-parrots on the stony islands of the far North.

"In the Village of Tukmeuk...

where a warm spring pours
into the sea and the water
never freezes in winter or
summer, there lived a lame
man named Kitmesuk.
Because he could not walk
long distances needed for
hunting, he made his living
at fishing.

Kitmesuk

Even though the water around Tukmeuk never froze, during the winter the ocean farther out did. Come springtime when the ice was breaking up on the ocean, he would take his kayak and go out in the channels of water between the floes. When he found what he thought would be a good place to fish he would climb out on a cake of ice

He placed a mat of willow branches on the ice, knelt down and peered into the clear water below. Then he would unwind a line from a short pole and fasten a bright bobber upon it. With his left hand, he would drop the bright bobber in the water and begin to bob it up and down. He held a long fish spear with his right hand.

When a salmon or salmon trout, thinking the bobber was something good to eat, would come round, he would spear him and put him on ice. He would catch many fish this way, which he would trade in the village for meat and deerskins to keep him warm.

One day Kitmesuk found a place which looked very good, so he began to bob the bright bobber in the water. But, though he bobbed until his wrist was sore and gripped his spear until his hand was nearly frozen, he saw no fish.

He was about to wind up his line and take up his mat, when he saw something moving in the water.

"Ah! Ah!" he whispered to himself, "Ah! Ho! and Ahneca! I will have my dinner from this pool, after all."

The thing in the water came closer. He lifted his spear to strike.

Had his spear come down, the creature must surely have died, for Kitmesuk was very sure with his spear. Just when he was ready to strike, he saw that this fish was not like any he had ever seen before.

"It appears to have a head like a man and feet behind its tail," he said to himself, in astonishment.

"Oh, well, it is a fish, and I am hungry. My eyes must be bad. After all it is but a fish."

Once more he threw back his arm. But just at that moment the creature shot straight up to the surface of the water.

Imagine the fisherman's surprise upon hearing a shrill voice saying:

"Do not spear me. I am not a fish. I am Fish-Boy."

Then Kitmesuk was angry. He guessed that Fish-Boy had been down there in the pool all the time. That was why he had caught no fish. Fish-Boy had frightened them off.

"Go away!"
he said angrily, "I want to catch some fish for my dinner."

"I do not wish to go away," said Fish-Boy. "I have no parents, and I am very lonely. I want you to be my father."

"But," said Kitmesuk in astonishment, "what use could you be to a poor man like me? You have no arms. A lame man may fish if he is not able to hunt. An armless fish-boy, he can do nothing at all except scare away the fish I need for my dinner and to trade in the village. No, no, go away!"

"I will not go away," replied Fish-Boy. "If you take me to be your son, I can be very useful to you. See if I am not. I will show you right now where there are some very large fish waiting to be caught."

On hearing this, Kitmesuk became interested in the curious boy. He helped him out of the water and dried him with a piece of soft sealskin.

"You are very small," he said.

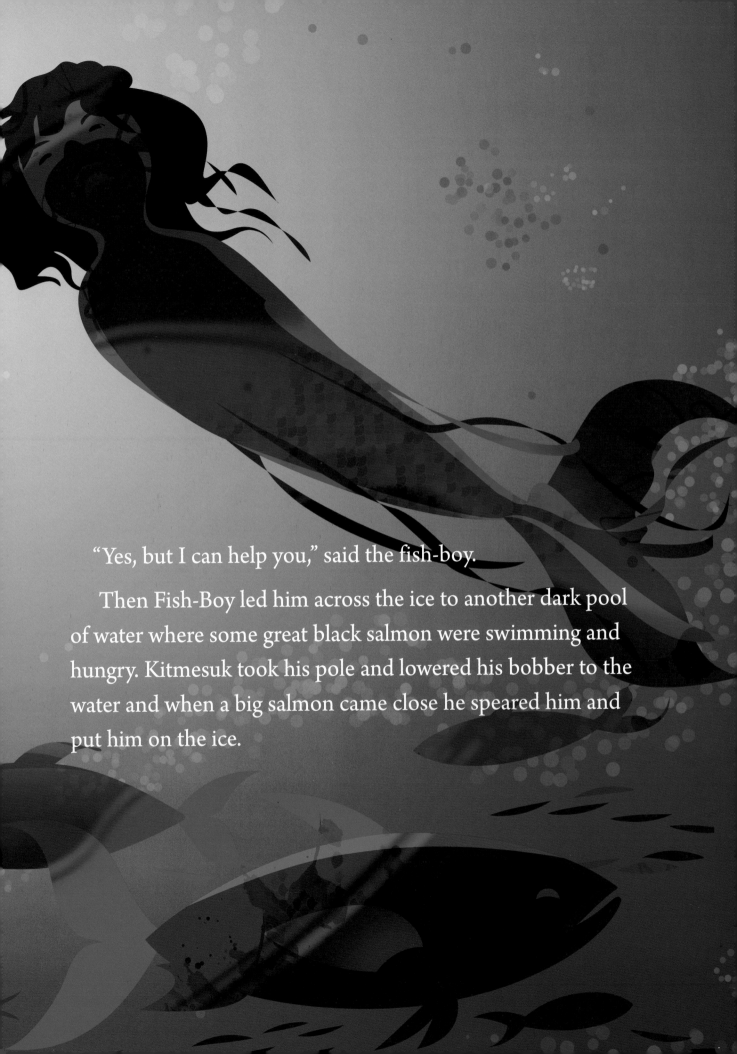

"Yes, but I can help you," said the fish-boy.

Then Fish-Boy led him across the ice to another dark pool of water where some great black salmon were swimming and hungry. Kitmesuk took his pole and lowered his bobber to the water and when a big salmon came close he speared him and put him on the ice.

When Kitmesuk returned home that night with his strange new son riding astride the back of his kayak, he had enough fish stowed away to feed them for a week.

They did this day after day. Fish-Boy would help Kitmesuk find the biggest fish and Kitmesuk would catch them and take his prizes back to the village. The people of Tukmeuk sang the praises of the great fisherman Kitmesuk and his son Fish-Boy.

It was no time at all until everyone up and down the coast, and even across the Narrow Waters, heard of Fish-Boy, son of Kitmesuk. Some came many miles to see them and their great catches.

Nepos-sok

Then one day...

Nepos-sok, chief of the great village across the Narrow Waters, heard of the old fisherman and his armless son. He sent a messenger with a splendid white-fox skin. The messenger said to Kitmesuk: "Here is a splendid fox skin. Nepos-sok gives you this beautiful skin as a present. He wishes to see your son."

But Kitmesuk would not accept the present. He did not wish to let Fish-Boy go across the Narrow Waters for fear that Nepos-sok would make him find fish for his village and not let him come back.

So the messenger came back to Nepos-sok and told him.

"Bring me my bag of skins," said the old chief.

"There," said he. "Take this to him." He held out a wonderful black sea-otter skin, six feet long. It was worth ten fox skins. "Tell Kitmesuk to take this as a present. I wish to see this fish-boy."

Then the messenger returned to Tukmeuk and presented the otter skin to Kitmesuk and repeated the chief's request to see his son.

Kitmesuk was about to refuse to accept this present also, when Fish-Boy said to him: "Why do you refuse to let me cross the Narrow Waters when I really wish to go?" If we can help feed this village with fish, should we not do so?"

"Oh! Do you wish to go? Why, then we will go."

So he accepted the present, and they started for the great village across the Narrow Waters. The messenger, who had gone before them, ran through the village, shouting. "Fish-Boy is coming! Fish-Boy is coming! The old fisherman and his armless son will be here soon."

So . . .

when Kitmesuk and Fish-Boy and the others arrived, the shore was filled with people. Everyone wanted to see this strange creature who had helped his father become a great fisherman. As soon as they stepped on shore everyone crowded about Fish-Boy, and nearly smothered him. Kitmesuk tried to keep them away, but Fish-Boy was calm and not scared.

Then the crowd pushed them along up the hill to their big singing house to see the old chief Nepos-sok. There it was much worse. The village people crowded on each other so that many were injured, some badly, and one man was almost killed.

Silly people that they were, they blamed Fish-Boy for their stupidity. Nepos-sok knew he could not keep this armless son of Kitmesuk around. So he sent at once for the village strong man to wrestle him and show that he was chief and his power was stronger than Fish-Boy's.

"Come," said the strong man to Fish-Boy, "you have caused injury to many of our chief's people. And because I am the strongest, if I catch you and throw you, I may kill you."

"But how am I to wrestle?" said Fish-Boy. "I have no arms." Even as he said this, however, he was not afraid.

"You must wrestle all the same," said the strong man, making a dash for him.

"All right, if you say so, we will wrestle," said Fish-Boy. Then he jumped high in the air and stayed there spinning around like a top. He looked down at the strong man and smiled. The crowd could not believe their eyes!

"Come down! And I will get you," shouted the strong man.

Fish-Boy floated down to the ground. But when the strong man made a second dash for him, he again jumped up and went spinning in the air.

This time, however, he came down upon the strong man's head and sent him sprawling across the floor.

With a terrible roar, the strong man sprang to his feet and leapt at Fish-Boy again.

But he was no more successful than before, and once again he was knocked sprawling.

When this had happened three times, he had had quite enough.

Now Nepos-sok came forward and said, "Go! And do not bother my village anymore! You have magic that must come from far, far away."

So Fish-Boy and Kitmesuk and the others got in their kayaks and paddled away.

These people were even more unfriendly than the others. Their strong man tried to shoot Fish-Boy with an arrow, but could not because of his wild hopping and spinning. So they broke up his boat, and said: "Now you and your father and his men may starve. We will give you nothing to eat."

"Come down to the beach," said Fish-Boy to his father and his men.

When they were on the beach he found the bills of some sea-parrots that had been killed by the villagers.

"Each of you take one and put it in your mouth," said Fish-Boy.

When they had all done this they were turned into sea-parrots. They flew up into the air and away from the St. Lawrence men.

When those villagers came down to the beach to see the strange thing that had happened —Ahneca!—they were caught by the strong magic and changed into sea-parrots!

And they too went fluttering…

and singing out over the water.

Then Fish-Boy led his father and men back to their homes. There he took away the strong magic and turned them all back into men again. But those wicked men of St. Lawrence Island, were never again turned back to men.

So, the great flocks of sea-parrots were once the awful men who refused kindness to Kitmesuk, the men from Tukmeuk and Fish-Boy.

"And that," said old Teragloona, striking the floor with his hunting knife, "is why there are so many sea-parrots skimming and singing over the ocean today."

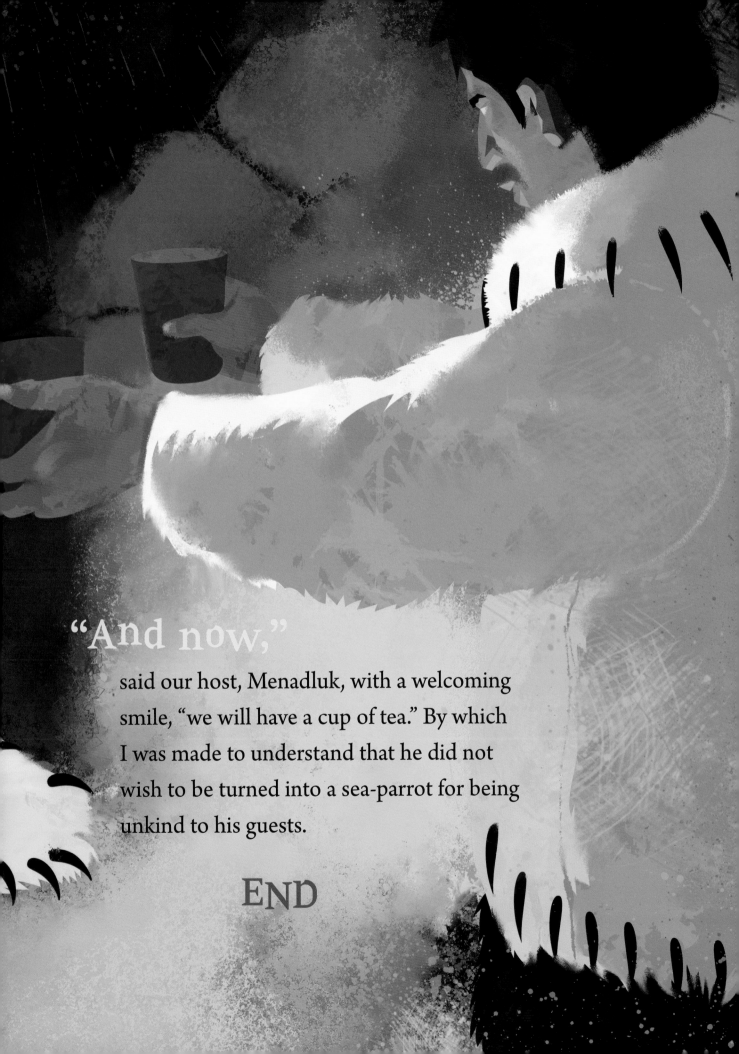

"And now," said our host, Menadluk, with a welcoming smile, "we will have a cup of tea." By which I was made to understand that he did not wish to be turned into a sea-parrot for being unkind to his guests.

END

New words for young readers.

Umiak

Ignaluk

Floes

Sea Parrot

Igloo

Ahneca! Hay naku has no direct translation. Some linguists say it comes from the phrase "Nanay ko po!" which means "Oh my mother!" Usage: Hay naku or hay nako is best said when you want to express frustration or exasperation in the likes of "Oh my," "Oh my gosh," "Oh dear," or "Uh oh!"

Diomedes Two small island between the United States and Russia, separated by the international date line (which, if you could stand there, you'd have one foot in today, one foot in tomorrow!). The Diomedes Islands are also known as Nunarbuk.

Floes Floating ice chunks on the surface of the sea. (singular: floe)

Igloo A shelter house made of blocks of hard snow or ice. Igloos are made in a dome shape.

Ignaluk The smaller of the two Diomedes Islands. (Also known as Little Diomedes)

Kayak A light, slender boat with pointed ends and a small opening for one person. It is usually covered with animal skins and rowed with a double-ended paddle.

Narrow Waters Before joining the Arctic Ocean, this is a small stretch of Pacific Ocean between Russia and the United States known as the Bering Strait. Scientists believe there was a "land bridge" here many years ago over which humans migrated, and from here, eventually populated all of the Americas).

Sea Parrot Known as the Atlantic puffin. They have penguin-like markings with a colorful beak. Sea parrots spend most of their time swimming and sitting on top of the water.

Singing Hall A place where the villagers can gather together to celebrate or mourn or make group decisions.

St. Lawrence Island Located in Alaska, it is the largest of the islands in the Bering Sea.

Umiak An open skin boat used by the Inuit, usually used to hunt, and holding up to 30 men. Like the kayak, it is made of driftwood and whalebone and covered by seal or walrus skins. The current-day Inuit still use these natural materials, for their prey is frightened away by the sounds of a metal boat.

Ahneca! A message for you.

I hope you enjoyed this Inuit legend. For creativity, try telling a story: how something came to be; why we do things the way we do; how things could/should be different (if ice cream was money; if gravity was turned off; if children were in charge).

–Vanita

Following are some interesting teaching points for readers:

- Hospitality
- Treatment of strangers
- Elder guidance
- Differently-abled people and how they are viewed and treated

- Killing for food and clothing
- Environment
- Telling stories that explain nature
- Teaching object lessons
- Transmitting values generationally

Vanita Oelschlager Author

VANITA is a wife, mother, grandmother, philanthropist, former teacher, current caregiver, author and poet. She is a graduate of the University of Mount Union in Alliance, Ohio, where she currently serves as a Trustee. Vanita is also Writer in Residence for the Literacy Program at The University of Akron. She and her husband Jim received a Lifetime Achievement Award from the National Multiple Sclerosis Society in 2006. She won the Congressional Angels in Adoption™ Award for the State of Ohio in 2007 and was named National Volunteer of the Year by the MS Society in 2008. She was honored as 2009 Woman Philanthropist of the Year by the United Way of Summit County. In May 2011, Vanita received an honorary Doctor of Humane Letters from the University of Mount Union. In 2013, Vanita joined The LeBron James Family Foundation to serve on its Advisory Board.

Mike Blanc Artist

Mike is an author and award-winning illustrator of children's literature. Books with Vanita include *The Gandy Dancers, The Pullman Porters, Postcards from a War* and *Bonyo Bonyo, The True Story of a Brave Boy from Kenya*, created with associate artist, Kristin Blackwood. In 2016, Mike wrote and illustrated *Cimarron Girl, The Dust Bowl Years of Abigail Brubaker*.

VanitaBooks Net Profits

VanitaBooks donates all net profits to charities where "people help people help themselves." Visit **www.VanitaBooks.com**. 10% of all net profits from this book will be donated to the Oak Clinic for Multiple Sclerosis. Oak Clinic's singular mission is to treat and empower individuals and families living with multiple sclerosis, regardless of their ability to pay. For information visit **www.oakclinic.com**.

Gateway to the North Pole

St. Lawrence Island

B E R I N G   S E A